The Flying Tree

Story by Julie Ellis

Illustrations by Naomi C. Lewis

Contents

Chapter 1	What a Mess!		2
Chapter 2	The Surprise		10
Chapter 3	Fly Away!		14

Chapter 1

What a Mess!

Emma and Matthew had come to stay with their gran and grandad for two nights.

"Oh, no!" cried Emma. "Look, Matthew! Our rocket ship tree has gone."

"Where is our rocket ship, Grandad?" asked Matthew.
"We were going to play on it."

"I'm sorry, children," said Grandad.
"The old tree had to go.
The leaves fell off and made a big mess.
So I got some men to cut it up
and take it away."

"We could help you clean up the mess,"
said Emma.

Matthew and Emma looked in the hole where the tree had been.

"I'm sad that our rocket ship tree has gone," said Emma.

"Cheer up," said Gran.
"Tomorrow, you will get a big surprise."

"What's the surprise?" asked Emma.

"Can we have a clue?" asked Matthew.

"The surprise is for you," said Grandad, "and it's going to go in the hole."

"Is it a sandpit?" asked Emma.

"Or a swimming pool?" asked Matthew.

"Wait and see," said Grandad.

Chapter 2

The Surprise

The next morning,
Matthew saw a truck stop at the gate.
On the back of it was something very big.

"Here's the surprise," he shouted.
"Come and look, Emma."

"It could be swings," said Emma,
running out to the gate.

"What is it, Grandad?" asked Matthew.

The driver pulled a cloth off the truck.
There was a very, **very** big tree.

"Can you put it in the hole, please?"
asked Grandad.

They watched as a crane lifted the tree
off the truck and put it into the hole.

"The tree looks like it's flying,"
laughed Emma.

Chapter 3

Fly Away!

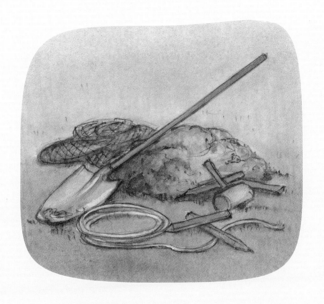

"It can be our flying tree," said Matthew.
"We can climb up into its branches
and fly away."

"You can't fly yet," smiled Grandad.
"The tree won't be ready for you to climb
until next holidays."

"The flying tree will be better than the rocket ship," said Emma.

"I'll be the captain and I'll take you to the moon," said Matthew.